EMMET'S AWESOME DAY

Written by Anna Holmes

Scholastic Children's Books
Euston House,
24 Eversholt Street,
London NW1 1DB, UK

A division of Scholastic Ltd
London ~ New York ~ Toronto ~ Sydney ~ Auckland
Mexico City ~ New Delhi ~ Hong Kong

This book was first published in the US in 2014 by Scholastic Inc.
Published in the UK by Scholastic Ltd, 2014

ISBN 978 1407 15569 2

Based on the Screenplay by PHIL LORD & CHRISTOPHER MILLER
Based on the Story by DAN HAGEMAN & KEVIN HAGEMAN and PHIL LORD & CHRISTOPHER MILLER
Special thanks to Katrine Talks and Matthew Ashton.

Printed and bound by L.E.G.O., Italy

2 4 6 8 10 9 7 5 3 1

One morning in the city of Bricksburg, Emmet Brickowski, the most ordinary guy in the world, woke up in his apartment.

Emmet did what he did every morning. He followed his book of instructions and showered, dressed, and ate breakfast while watching his favourite TV show, *Where Are My Pants?* Then he drove to work.

What Emmet didn't know was that today was going to be the most extraordinary day of his life.

Emmet worked for a construction company that tore down quirky buildings and replaced them with tall, identical skyscrapers.

No one knew why the buildings needed to be demolished. Those were just President Business's instructions.

And the best way to fit in, have everyone like you, and always be happy was to follow President Business's instructions.

As Emmet was leaving work that evening, he noticed something strange. A mysterious person was digging through the debris at the building site.

"Hey, pal," Emmet called, "I don't think you're supposed to be here."

The intruder turned and Emmet gasped. It was a girl, and she was beautiful!

Startled, Emmet lost his footing. He slipped down the pile of rubble and fell into a deep, dark hole! When Emmet finally landed, a strange, red, object was glowing in front of him. It was unlike anything he'd ever seen.

"I feel like maybe I should touch that," Emmet said. And when he did, a bright, white light flashed, and he passed out.

When Emmet woke up, he was handcuffed to a chair.

"How did you find the Piece of Resistance?" a voice bellowed at him. It was Bad Cop.

"I don't know what you're talking about," Emmet insisted. Then he saw that the weird, red object was attached to his back! "How did that get there?" Emmet cried.

"Playing dumb, Master Builder?" Bad Cop sneered. "Why else would you show up just three days before President Business is going to use the Kragle to end the world?"

Bad Cop ordered his police robots to take Emmet to the melting chamber and remove the strange piece!
Emmet was sure he was a goner. But then the mysterious girl from the building site broke in and fought off the robots. "Come with me if you wanna *not* die!" she said to Emmet.

Quickly, Emmet and the girl escaped into an alleyway. Emmet watched in awe as she pulled random pieces from the alley to build an awesome motorbike ... without any instructions!

"Who are you?" he asked.

"I'm Wyldstyle," she said. "I'm rescuing you, sir."

Emmet was so confused. "Will you please tell me what is happening?"

"You're the one the prophecy spoke of," Wyldstyle said. "You found the Piece of Resistance. That means you're the Special. The prophecy states that you are the most interesting and important person in the universe. That's you, right?"

Emmet thought for a moment. "Uh … yes. That's me."

Wyldstyle explained that President Business was actually the evil Lord Business. He was planning to use a super weapon called the Kragle to glue the world together.

The only thing that could stop him was the strange piece attached to Emmet's back. According to the prophecy, that meant Emmet was destined to save the world.

Just then, Wyldstyle drove the motorbike through a secret portal and they crashed into another realm called the Wild West!

Wyldstyle took Emmet to a saloon to meet Vitruvius, a blind wizard. He was the leader of the Master Builders: a team of super-creative people that could build anything without following instructions!

Vitruvius was very excited that Emmet had found the Piece of Resistance. But Emmet wasn't sure he was "the Special."

"The prophecy chose you, Emmet," Vitruvius said. "All you have to do is believe."

Suddenly, Bad Cop and his robots blasted into the saloon! Emmet, Wyldstyle, and Vitruvius escaped on a flying machine and headed toward the edge of the realm.

Bad Cop chased after them in his flying police car. With one well-aimed blaster shot, he knocked them out of the sky. Now Emmet was *sure* he was a goner.

As they were falling through the air, Emmet wanted to tell Wyldstyle he was sorry he hadn't been able to save the world. But just before he could get the words out, a sleek, bat-shaped plane swooped in and saved them.

"Relax everybody, I'm here." It was Batman!

In a flash, Batman flew everyone to Cloud Cuckoo Land: a realm perched on a cloud at the top of a rainbow.

There, they were greeted by someone very energetic and positively perky. "*Hiyee!* I'm Princess UniKitty. And I'll take you to the Master Builders."

This realm was the wackiest, most-colourful world Emmet had ever seen. UniKitty had definitely not used instructions to build this place!

When the Master Builders met Emmet, they were doubtful he could help them defeat Lord Business. He did not look special!

Emmet took a deep breath. "Yes, it's true, I may not be a Master Builder. And I know what you're thinking: He is the least-qualified person to lead us."

That made the Master Builders even more upset. But before Emmet could explain that he was going to do his best, a giant golf ball crashed through the window.

It was Bad Cop again! He had put a tracking device on Emmet in the Wild West and followed them to Cloud Cuckoo Land.

"Take the Master Builders prisoner!" Bad Cop ordered his police robots.

Emmet gasped. Because of him, Cloud Cuckoo Land was under attack and all the Master Builders were in danger!

"Come on, everyone!" Wyldstyle cried. "Protect the Special!"

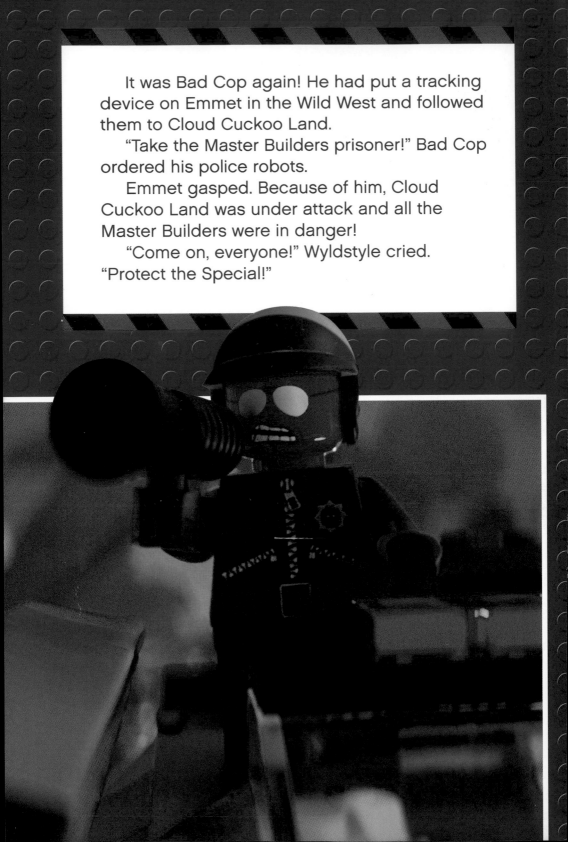

Wyldstyle, Vitruvius, UniKitty, Batman, and a spaceman named Benny quickly built a wacky submarine to escape underwater.

Emmet wanted to help, but the only creative thing he had ever thought to build without instructions was a Double-Decker Couch. So he built that.

With a giant splash, the friends plunged into the water. But it wasn't long before the submarine began to flood. The friends only had one choice – they jumped on top of Emmet's Double-Decker Couch and floated to safety.

Emmet couldn't believe it. His invention had saved them! Perhaps he did have what it took to be the Special after all.

Another Master Builder named Metal Beard came to rescue them on his pirate ship. "Avast, maties!" he called.

Dry and safe onboard, Emmet realized it was up to him to come up with a plan to stop Lord Business. He might not feel like the Special, but the Master Builders were counting on him.

"What's the last thing Lord Business expects Master Builders will do?" Emmet asked.

His friends shrugged. They had no idea.

"It's follow the instructions!" Emmet cried.

Following Emmet's instructions, the heroes built a spaceship just like the ones Lord Business's robots used. Inside it, they were able to sneak into Lord Business's evil office tower!

Emmet and Wyldstyle crept to the Kragle room while the others went to shut off the security system.

Just outside, Emmet paused. There was something he wanted Wyldstyle to know.

"That night in the city," he said, "when you thought I was the Special, that was the first time anyone had ever really told me that. It made me want to do everything I could to be the guy you were talking about."

Wyldstyle was touched. Emmet's words meant a lot to her. "Good luck, Emmet," she said.

A moment later, the laser beams protecting the Kragle dropped. The others had done it – the security field was down!

But just as Emmet was about to place the Piece of Resistance on top of the weapon, he saw something terrible.

Bad Cop was right behind Wyldstyle!

Lord Business laughed maniacally as he marched into the room. His robots had captured the other Master Builders, too. Their mission was a failure.

Lord Business removed the Piece of Resistance from Emmet's back and threw it out the window!

Without the Piece of Resistance, there was no way to stop the Kragle, now.

Lord Business tied Emmet to a battery linked to an explosive device. It was set to destroy the tower – and all the Master Builders captured in it.

"Well, I guess there's only one thing left to do," Lord Business said. "Release the Kragle!"

Lord Business rose into the air on his flying machine, along with the Kragle. In a blinding flash of light, he zoomed off, prepared to glue the world together.

As the explosive-device timer ticked down, Emmet looked at his friends. He couldn't believe this was the end.

And then, all at once, Emmet realized what he needed to do. It wasn't the best idea he had ever had. But it was the most important.

Using all his strength, Emmet wiggled over to the window along with the battery tied to his back … and jumped out! The wires snapped, deactivating the device.

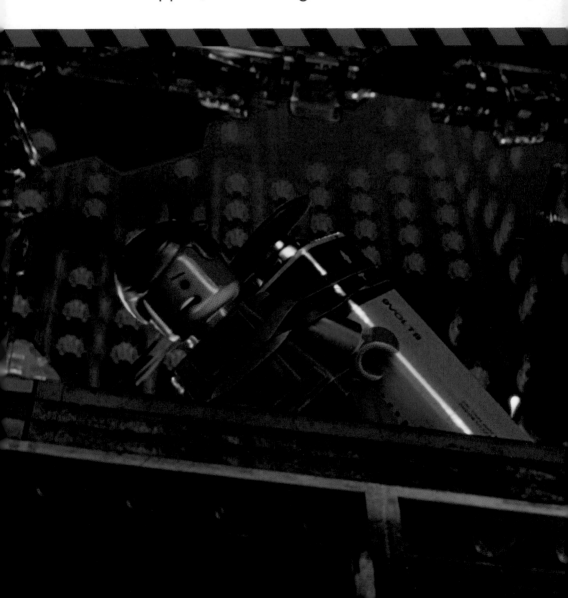

Instantly, the computer shut down and the Master Builders were freed!

But Emmet was gone. Wyldstyle was heartbroken.

"Arr," said Metal Beard sadly. "If only there were more people in the world like he."

Wyldstyle looked at the monitors showing Lord Business freezing everyone in Bricksburg. Suddenly, she gasped. "Maybe there are."

Using Lord Business's own television cameras, the Master Builders sent a message out to everyone in all the realms. Wyldstyle told them about Emmet, and his sacrifice. "Now we have to finish what he started, by making whatever weird thing pops into our heads," she said. "We need to fight back against President Business's plans to freeze us!"

Meanwhile, Emmet fell and fell and fell. For a while, he thought he was going to fall forever.

When he finally landed, something was not right. The world around him didn't look … normal. And he couldn't move!

Suddenly, a little boy named Fynn picked him up.

Fynn told Emmet that his father was trying to glue all the LEGO pieces – Emmet's world – together. But the boy didn't want that to happen.

He handed Emmet the Piece of Resistance. It was the cap to the glue tube.

"It's up to you now, Emmet," he said.

Emmet crash-landed back in Bricksburg, and a huge smile broke over his face. He could *see* how to build awesome things without following the instructions for the first time, just like a Master Builder!

In the blink of an eye, Emmet built a super machine and flew to Lord Business's Kraglizer.

"You're too late, Brickowski!" Lord Business yelled.

Emmet shook his head. "I'm going to unleash my secret weapon. Here it comes…"

Emmet held out his hand. "It's called the power of the Special. It's my hand. I want you to take it."

Emmet realized that, just like the boy's father, Lord Business wanted to be in control. But deep down, what he really wanted was to feel special.

"You don't have to be the bad guy," Emmet said. "Look at all these things that people built. You might see a mess. What I see are people, inspired by one another, and by you. Because you are the Special. And so is everyone."

Lord Business was speechless. No one had ever said that to him before. It made him feel different. Changed. "Thank you."

Emmet had convinced Lord Business to stop gluing everything together and to place the Piece of Resistance on top of the Kragle.

Emmet had saved the world.

Down below, the people cheered. Emmet's friends were overjoyed to see he was alive, especially Wyldstyle.

"Emmet!" she cried running up to hug him. "You did it!"

Emmet grinned. He had done it, but certainly not alone. If it hadn't been for his friends and the little boy named Fynn, he couldn't have done any of it.

This had turned out to be the most incredible, most extraordinary, most exciting day of Emmet's life. And as he watched the people of Bricksburg cheering, and saw all of the amazing things they had built without following the instructions, he had a feeling that there were many more awesome days ahead.